by AJ Stern • illustrated by Doreen Mulryan Marts

SCHOLASTIC INC.
New York Toronto London Auckland
Sydney Mexico City New Delhi Hong Kong

ISBN 978-0-545-38787-3

 Published by Scholastic Inc., 557 Broadway, New York, NY 10012, by arrangement with Grosset & Dunlap, a division of Penguin Young Readers Group, a member of Penguin Group (USA) Inc.

12 11 10 9 8 7 6 5 4 3 2 1 11 12 13 14 15 16/0

Printed in the U.S.A. 40

This edition first printing, September 2011

CHAPTER 1

It is a **scientific fact** that I had three **fantastical** ideas in one day. It all started the morning I returned Herbert, our class rabbit. Everyone gets a chance to take him home for one entire night. When it was my turn, our teacher, Mrs. Pellington, said, "Frannie, do *not* do anything with Herbert other than feed him, watch him, and clean his cage."

I looked Mrs. Pellington right

in the eyeballs and promised her I would not do ***any*** of her ***Do Nots***. It is a good thing she said something because I was going to practice a new haircutting style on Herbert.

I'm so good at cutting hair; I am considering being a professional haircutter. The only thing is, I don't think they have offices and if you don't already know this about me, I love offices.

When I returned Herbert the next day without any haircuts or even **seventeen-one-hundred** teeny tiny ponytails all over him (which is **a for instance** of a new style I'm working on) Mrs. P. was so **impresstified** that she said in front of my entire class, "Frannie, I'm extremely proud of you. You are clearly very good with animals."

Clearly and **extremely** are very grown-up words. I try and use adult words as oftenly as possible.

My best friend, Elliott, was clearly extremely happy for me because when I looked over at him, he gave me a double thumbs-up. My smile was so big, it almost wrapped around my entire head. And that is when I had my first **fantastical** idea.

My dad always says people should put their talents to good use. Certainly, I hadn't realized I was so talented with animals, but once I found out I was, I planned to put it to good use. So I decided to un-become a haircutter and become a veterinarian, instead. Although I'd never been to a veterinarian before, I knew for an actual fact that they had offices. I knew because my parents **actually** *know* a veterinarian. Dr. Katz. In my head, I spell it *Dr. Cats*, but it is a **scientific fact** that he spells it with a K. And a Z.

And if you didn't know this about me, you should probably also know that last week, I had planned on being our mayor's assistant. But he **actually** never called me after I sent him my résumé. (A résumé is a list of all the offices you've worked at.) So my parents said I should think about other jobs.

During recess, I told Elliott that I was changing jobs. He asked me if he could be a doctor with me at my veterinarian's office. I told him no, because I really needed a secretary.

Then his eyes nearly flew out of his head, across the room, down the stairs, and out the door. "I have *always* wanted to be a veterinarian secretary!" he said, even though I knew that was not a **scientific fact**.

Last week, Elliott wanted to be the assistant to the assistant (me!) of the mayor and yesterday he wanted to be an assistant to a haircutter (also me)! That is because (and I am not saying this in a bragging type of way) Elliott likes to copy a lot of things I do. Wanting to have a job is just one of those things he copies. It's okay with me because my father says Elliott's copying is a compliment.

And also because he only wants to be an assistant.

"We can practice when you come visit me!" I said. Elliott was staying at my house this weekend because his parents were going out of town.

The timing couldn't have been more **extremely** or **clearly** perfect.

CHAPTER

When I got home, I was bursting out of my own skin to tell everyone my good news. That's why instead of yelling out "I'm home!" I yelled, "I'm a veterinarian!"

I ran up the stairs, down the hall, and into my room. I had an **incredible, extremely** plan. I was going to open my own veterinarian's office in my bedroom. If I wanted it to be ready in time for Elliott's visit on Friday, which was the day after tomorrow, I needed to get busy. Since I had never been to a veterinarian's office before, I had to take some good guesses at what one would be like.

I took all my stuffed animals off my bed and put them next to each other on the floor. They were now officially sitting in the waiting room.

I didn't know if veterinarians wore stethoscopes, but I was going to be the type of veterinarian who did. I opened my sock drawer and pulled out a pair of tights. I put them around my neck with one leg draping down each side. I tied the feet together to look like the round part at the bottom of the stethoscope.

I pushed my desk to the center of the room because that was the examining table. Then I moved one chair next to it. That's where I would sit and take doctor notes on all the animals' complaints. Okay, maybe the **actual** animals wouldn't complain, but their owners would! I put another chair on the far side of the room where Elliott would sit as my secretary.

I pulled out some paper and drew a lot of dog bones on them, then cut them up very carefully, putting each bone picture in front of all the waiting dogs so they didn't get hungry.

I was only going to be a dog veterinarian. Cats are too slippy. Every time I try to hug one, they always spill out of my arms. That is why I was only going to have dog patients.

I sat down and looked around. What was missing? A doctor's coat!

I heard my parents talking in the kitchen so I knew the coast was clear. Then I ran down the hall and into their bedroom, where I took a white, button-down shirt off of one of my dad's hangers. That would be my doctor coat. **I** put it on, and **with** the tights hanging around my neck, **I** looked **actually** and **clearly** like the most professional dog veterinarian anyone has ever seen!

Back in my room, I made the official sign for the office:

I practiced listening to the dogs' hearts. But after a while, it was boring.

I needed to practice on real animals. In a real veterinarian's office. And the only way to do that was to **actually** work for a real veterinarian.

And that is when I had my second **fantastical** idea. I was going to retire from school and work for Dr. Katz! I *already* had a résumé. I just had to think of the perfect way to get my parents to agree.

CHAPTER

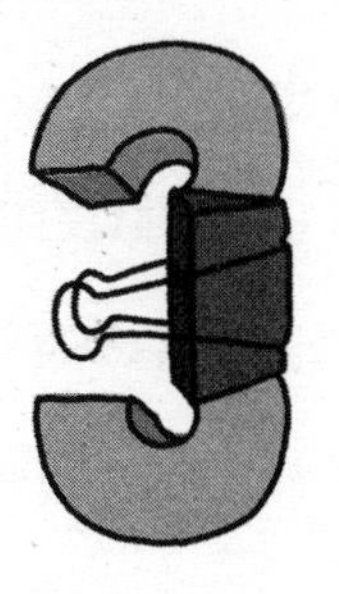

That night at dinner, I told my parents I had a lot of news. I was going to tell them in size order. Smallest news first, biggest news last.

"I have opened a dog veterinarian's office on the second floor. It's for live dogs, not stuffed ones. That is really a problem because I don't have any live dogs," I told them during the salad part of dinner.

This was the part where they were

supposed to get their own fantastical idea. My mom was supposed to say, "Well, maybe you could take some time off from school and work for Dr. Katz. What do you think, Dan?"

And my dad was supposed to answer, "I was just going to say the same thing!"

But my dad just said, "That *is* a problem!"

"We only have stuffed animals in this house," I continued. My parents looked at me with twisty smiles at their mouth corners.

"Those are good observations, Frannie," my dad said.

"I wonder if there is a kind of place that is not a zoo where there are a lot of animals. That would be a good place for me to go work at being a dog veterinarian since I actually and clearly can't do it here. You really need live dogs if you're going to practice being a dog veterinarian. You can't do that at the zoo because there aren't any dogs at the zoo. I wonder where you can do that. Do you happen to know?" I asked both my parents.

This was the part where they were supposed to suggest that I give up school and work for Dr. Katz. But they didn't do that here, either! All they did was this:

"A place that's not a zoo," my dad said, scrunching his eyebrows together. "I'll have to think on that."

"It would have to be a place where there were doctors and animals. A place where the doctors were the doctors *for* the animals, but again—

not a zoo. That is the exact type of place I need to work at. But, if I worked at a place like that, I probably wouldn't have much time for school."

"Okay, Frannie. Like I said, we'll think on it." Then my dad turned to my mom and said, "Did you hear that Bill and Janice are going to Italy for two weeks?"

"I did!" my mom said. "Rome . . . It's so exciting!"

Oh no! What was happening? The conversation was changing. If they didn't think I was serious about working for Dr. Katz, they'd never let me do it! The only way to prove my **seriousity** was to show them how much I know about dogs.

"Did you know that dogs come in all different sizes?" I interrupted.

"Even in Rome," I added so they didn't think I was too **interruptish**.

"I did," my dad said, helping himself to some spaghetti. "Just like people," he added.

"Some dogs are so little, you can carry them around in your pocket and you don't even have to walk them!"

"Is that so?" my mom asked, taking a sip of her seltzer water. **It** is a **scientific fact** that seltzer is a grown-up version of water.

"It *is* so. Did you also know that there are one thousand million different types of dogs? Someone at my school has a dog that is half poodle and half a different kind of dog and it is called a *Labradoodle*."

"A Labradoodle! What a funny name!" my mom said.

"Like I said, there are one thousand million different types of dogs. Labradoodle is just one of them. I certainly know a lot more types."

"I didn't know you were quite so informed about dogs, Frannie!" my mom said, **impresstified**. This was working!

"I am. I'm quite informed. Mrs. Pellington said I'm very good with animals. A natural." I added the part about being a natural. "My favorite types of dogs are Goldendoodles and Sheep Poodles."

I didn't actually know if these were real types of dogs, but when you're as good and natural with animals as I am, you're **probably usually** right.

"I also really like Skeedaddles and Puffdoodles."

"Wow, I've never heard of those types of dogs. Are you sure you're not making these up?" my dad asked with a small twinkle in his eye that said, *even if you are making these up, you seem so responsible and smart about dogs, if you happen to ask us if you can quit school to get a job as a veterinarian's assistant, we will say yes.*

I told them a little about Schnoodles and Bageegles but when my mom turned to my dad to say something else about Rome, I stood up.

Sometimes you need to stand up to make announcements.

"I am sorry to interrupt, but I have something to tell you and it's very, extremely . . . official." My parents looked at me with their waiting faces. I was quiet for a minute and that's when I realized I'd need to use my English accent. English accents are very professional.

"Ahyve desoyded to ree-tiyah from school becawzz I am gowing to woohk for Dawktah Kaaatz," I announced in my absolute, **extremely professional** English accent.

I waited for them to respond, but

they didn't say anything. They just sat there with very confused expressions. That's when I realized they didn't understand my English accent because it was *too* amazing! They probably needed me to repeat it without the accent.

"I have decided to retire from school because I am going to work for Dr. Katz," I said in my regular voice.

But instead of saying "Let me call school right now and cancel!" or "That is the best and most professional idea we've ever heard!" my dad just covered my hand with his and said, "Frannie, you are a true original."

"You sure are, Frannie," my mom agreed. I learned the hard way that **original means one-of-a-kind**. One-of-a-kind is good if you are a person, but bad if you are wet paper. Especially when the original paper has **extremely professional** office words on it. And gets ruined because someone spilled something on it. Which is **a for instance** of something I did by accident when I was a kid one month ago.

These were not the reactions I wanted. When I opened my mouth to say more, the phone rang.

My mom hates it when people call during dinner, but I love when people call, no matter when. That's because when I answer the phone, my parents let me say, "Miller residence, this is Frannie. How may I direct your call?" Because that's how I've heard office people answer. But I was not allowed to pick up the phone during dinner.

The phone stopped ringing for a few seconds and then it rang again. Then it stopped and started again one more time and my parents gave each other emergency looks.

When someone keeps calling, it usually means something is wrong!

CHAPTER 4

When the person called back a third time, my dad rushed out of his seat and picked up the phone. We could only hear his end of the conversation and it went like this:

"Oh no! That's terrible. What happened? Uh-huh, uh-huh, you're kidding! Of course! Really? That's so exciting! Don't be silly. We'd be happy to do it. Oh, she'll love that!"

My mom and I looked at each

other. How can something be terrible and exciting at the same time?

"Okay, will do. We'll see you soon," my dad said.

When my dad sat back down, he looked upset.

"What is it, Dan?"

"Magoo broke her leg." Magoo is my dad's sister, which makes her my aunt. Her real name is Margot, but instead of saying that name when I was a baby, I said "Magoo." So it stuck.

"How?"

My dad looked right at me when he said the answer.

"She tripped over her dog!"

I could not believe my own eardrums! **In a million, trillion years** I would never trip over my dog. And that is **not an opinion**.

“So, what’s the exciting part?” asked my mom.

This question really **excitified** my father. "A fancy New York toy store owner wants to look at Magoo's sock dolls. She's thinking of ordering a whole bunch of them!"

Magoo makes dolls out of socks. They are really cute and funny with buttons for eyes and yarn for hair. They are called sock dolls because they're made from socks stuffed with cotton. Some are plaid and polka-dotted. Some are striped. And others have lots of curly lines on them. I am really lucky because I have three. I can even make one myself. Magoo showed me how.

"But since she broke her leg she needs our help getting ready for the meeting."

That was when I remembered a **really important scientific fact**.

"But she's all the way in Massachusetts!" I told my father. "Which is really far from Chester."

"We'll have a road trip!" he said.

"But, Elliott!" I said before getting the terrible **disappointment drop** in my belly. "Will he be able to come with us?"

"He's more than welcome," my mom

said. That brought a big smile to my face, but I was sad we wouldn't get to use the practice veterinarian's office right away. "Let me call his parents and run it by them," she said, getting out of her seat.

"I left out the best for last," my dad said.

I looked up.

"Magoo has a job for you and it has to do with her pets! I'll let her tell you herself, but it sure sounded like the perfect job for a budding veterinarian!"

I was so **excitified**, my brains almost fell into my spaghetti. I was going to show my parents that I was ready to work for Dr. Katz and quit school. I was going to show them by being really good with Bark,

Magoo's dog. Magoo also had three slippy cats—Hester, Esther, and Lester—but I'd let Elliott watch them because I was only a dog veterinarian. And that was my third **fantastical** idea in exactly one full day.

CHAPTER 5

It didn't feel like a long drive to Magoo's on Friday afternoon because as soon as Elliott and I got in the car, we fell asleep. What did take a long time was waiting for Magoo to answer the door!

We heard her yell, "I'm coming!"

But then we waited and the door still didn't open.

"Hang on! I'm almost there!" she called again.

Elliott and I looked at each other

and giggled. Adults are really weird sometimes. We heard lots of messing around with the doorknob and finally Magoo opened the door.

Have you ever seen more than one really exciting thing at the exact same time and then you can't decide which thing to look at first? That is the **exact same** thing that happened to me!

Here is the blur of what happened. When Magoo opened the door, the first thing I saw was a cast that went all the way past her knee and up her thigh! But before I could even study it, Bark ran past Magoo, put his paws on my shoulders, and knocked me over. Elliott backed away really quickly because he got scared, and that is **not an opinion**.

Bark licked my face over and over with his pink, sloppy tongue. I squinched my eyes and mouth and turned my head away because **I do not** like being licked on the face. I really hoped getting your face licked was **not** part of being a veterinarian. I also hoped that Magoo and my parents didn't see me squinching. I needed them to think I was a natural with animals. Dogs especially!

"Bark must have really missed you," Magoo said.

My dad pulled me up and I tried to wait until Bark turned his head before I wiped his licks off my face. I didn't want to hurt his feelings.

Besides the licking that I didn't like, there was so much about Bark I did like. **A for instance of what I**

mean is that Bark has the softest hair and it feels just like fluff. He is white all over his body and has gray spots on the top parts of himself. He's very shaggy and always looks like he needs a haircut, but he doesn't. That's the way his hair is supposed to look. I know that

because once I tried to cut it off and Magoo caught me just in time to explain about shaggy dog hair.

"He's a Labradinger, right?" I asked Magoo. Now was my chance to show her how much I knew about dogs!

"No, just a plain old sheepdog," she said. She was certainly not right about that. I knew a **Labradinger** when I saw one. Then I remembered about introducing people.

"This is my best friend, Elliott."

Elliott and Magoo shook hands and Magoo said, "Elliott, I don't know if you want a job as much as my niece does, but if you do, you're in luck."

"I do," Elliott said, excited, but then his face dropped a little. "But I already have a job. I'm Frannie's secretary."

My parents and Magoo laughed out loud, and Elliott and I looked at each other confused. Sometimes grown-ups don't know the difference between **funny** things and **not funny** things.

"Well, if Frannie will let you, I'd like to offer you the job of special assistant to cats."

Elliott looked at me and I looked at Magoo.

"Would he still get to be my secretary?" I asked Magoo.

"Absolutely," Magoo told me.

I looked back at Elliott and said, "Okay, you can take that job."

Then Magoo said, "Great, now come on in." She opened the door even wider. And that is when I saw that Magoo's cast was the most exciting one I had ever seen. It didn't have one single drawing or name on it like when kids got casts. It was perfectly clean and white and actually very **super extra professional-looking**. I couldn't take my eyes off it. But when Magoo took her crutches out from under her armpits and hopped to the side to get out of our way, I couldn't take my eyes off the crutches! They were the **most special** crutches I'd seen in the entire world of America. They were not wooden like the ones kids used; they were metal, which meant they were silver! Everyone knows that silver things are **very adult**.

Magoo's cast and crutches made her look very official. I wanted to reach my arm out toward them, but my dad saw inside my brain because just as I was reaching out for them, he said, “Don’t even think about it.”

I quickly pulled my arm away.

"How in the worldwide did you know what I was thinking?"

"I have special mind-reading dad powers," he said, even though **I knew that was not actually a scientific fact**.

We followed Magoo as she crutched her way around her house while we pointed out different things to Elliott. I had already been to Magoo's house so I felt very smart about everything that was there.

"What are those?" Elliott asked, pointing to the wall of shelves where her dolls lived.

"Those are my sock dolls," Magoo said.

"Oh yeah! Frannie has some in her room," said Elliott.

"Would you like to see one?" Magoo asked.

Elliott nodded his head up, down, up, down, like it was a horse on the merry-go-round. Magoo crutched over to the shelf.

"A boy one!" Elliott requested.

She brought back a boy sock doll and Elliott studied it very closely, turning it around and around. He investigated the striped legs and polka-dot arms, the button eyes and the thick, brown nose stitches. He pulled gently on the thick, brown yarn that was cut short into boy hair. Then he looked up with an expression I'd never seen before.

"Are there any sock doll makers that are boys?" he asked Magoo.

"I believe there are, Elliott."

"Well, could I be a special assistant to cats, Frannie's secretary, *and* a boy sock doll maker?"

Magoo beamed. "I don't see why not!"

"Elliott!" I said.

"What?"

"I think that is too many jobs . . ."

"Why?" he asked.

"Because it is against the law to have so many."

"Oh," he said. I could not believe **for the worldwide life of me** that he didn't know that.

He thought for a minute.

"Maybe I can be a sock doll maker and special assistant to cats on weekends, and then your secretary during the week?"

I thought about this for **one**

point two moments and then I agreed to what sounded like a very good deal.

"I can't wait to show you how to make them!" Magoo told him.

Elliott handed the doll back to Magoo. "Thanks for showing it to me."

"You can hold on to it for now, if you want."

"I can?" Elliott could hardly believe his **worldwide** luck. I didn't feel badly because, like I said, I already owned three sock dolls.

We walked around Magoo's house a little more. There's always so much to investigate there because there are so many rooms. **A for instance of what I mean** is that she has a craft room, a sunroom, and a meditation room. That's a room for being quiet. Elliott and I were not so interested in that room. Plus, she has a gift closet, a television room, a playroom where the animals sleep, and then all the usual rooms.

I can tell my mom likes the quiet room the best because she popped her head in and said, "Oh, Magoo. It's marvelous what you've done with this space!"

Marvelous is a grown-up word, but it's not for me. It's very old-fashioned.

Elliott and I felt really lucky because we were going to sleep on couches in the sunroom. A sunroom is a room that is outside, like a porch, but has a screen on it, so that it is also inside. The sun gets to come into the room and that is the **scientific fact** for how it got its name.

The cats meowed and rubbed up against my leg. I looked down, but I was not going to pick any of them up because I could tell just looking at them that they were the extra slippy kind of cat. I also wanted Magoo to see that I was a natural with dogs—not cats!

"What are the cats' names?" Elliott asked Magoo.

"Hester, Esther, and Lester," she said.

See what I mean about slippy? Slippy names for slippy cats.

CHAPTER 6

After settling in, we had a meeting. It was the most **boringest** meeting I'd ever been to. Elliott, too. I doodled in my head and passed notes to Elliott using just my brain waves. I knew he was doing it, too, because we got **boringified** at the same things. The only time it was not boring was when Magoo explained about the fancy toy store person.

"She's in town for only one day

and she is very interested in looking at my sock dolls because she might want to sell them in her store."

"It's just so exciting," my mom said. I could tell she really meant it because her eyes looked very sparkly.

"They have sock doll stores?" Elliott asked with his mouth wide open.

Magoo laughed. "It's more like a store that sells lots of toys and dolls. They've never sold this type of doll there before. But they're interested in looking at mine!"

Elliott and I looked at each other with **WOW** eyes.

"The point is," Magoo said, "this woman is coming to town especially to meet me. Since my leg is broken, she's offered to come here to see me instead of having me come to New York City with all my dolls. Now here's the very important part . . ." Elliott and I leaned in to make sure we didn't miss the very important part. "The toy store woman is very, very allergic to cats. Because I have three cats, we have to start cleaning very early on Sunday. We need to vacuum everywhere and close the cats up in the TV room. We have to make her visit as comfortable and itch-free as possible. There can't be cat hair anywhere."

"Do we get to come to the meeting?" I asked.

"Unfortunately, no," Magoo said. **Unfortunately** is a good grown-up word I needed to use more. "But, you *are* going to go in the car with your dad to pick her up on Sunday!"

"Fun!" I said. Elliott agreed.

"The most important thing is that there cannot be one single cat hair in this house."

Then my dad talked and told Elliott how to feed the cats. His instructions sounded like this: *Boring boring boring. Boring boring boring. A little more boring. Even* ***boringer****. One last time with the* ***boringest*** *of boring until finally, your ears close shut so you never have to hear anything boring again.*

"We all clear?" my dad asked. Everyone nodded yes. "Good, then let's get to work. This house needs to be in tip-top order for Magoo's big meeting, and Bark needs to be walked."

That was my cue. While Elliott went into the kitchen to open the smelly bag of cat food, I went and got Bark's leash from the front hall table. Then, I went over and clipped it to Bark's collar like a professional leasher!

That is when Magoo said, with a big *I forgot something* in her voice, "Oh, shoot—Frannie!" I looked up. "I forgot to tell you your job title."

I was so **excitified** to hear my title, I held my breath.

"I was so busy telling Elliott about his job, I forgot to tell you about yours. *You* are the president of cats."

Cats?

My mouth fell off my entire face.

"But, I am going to be a *DOG* veterinarian," I said. "Not a cat one."

"I know, sweetie," Magoo said. "But Bark is just too big for you."

"No, he's not too big. He's the perfect size," I said. And just when I said that, Bark jumped up on me and knocked me down.

"Sorry, sweetie. Maybe next year when you're bigger."

Next year? Next year I wasn't even going to want to be a dog veterinarian!

"Sorry, Bird," my dad said, taking the leash from me. Bird is my middle name. Please do not tell anyone. **It** is a **scientific fact** that my dad is the only one who calls me by it.

I looked over at Elliott in the kitchen. He was lining up three boring cat bowls. I looked back down at Bark. If I wasn't taking care of Bark, how would I prove that I was ready to be a dog veterinarian?

I dragged myself into the kitchen and helped Elliott pour the stinky food into the boring bowls. As my dad tugged on Bark's leash, Bark looked over at me and I could tell by his expression that he wished I were the one taking care of him. His eyes were very droopy, which meant he was sad, and his breathing was very fast and heavy, which meant he was getting sadder by the second! I looked over at my mom on the couch to make sure she saw how sad Bark was to leave me. But she was too unfortunately busy picking a piece of cat fur off her sweater to see the tragedy.

When my dad and Bark left for their walk, Elliott and I finished feeding and watering the cats. Then I **harrumphed** around and Magoo taught Elliott how to make sock dolls.

That night before we got into our couch beds, I did something to show Magoo how thoughtful and responsible I was. I hoped it would make her change her mind and switch my job with my dad's job.

Sometimes when you go to Disney World and stay at their hotel, the housekeepers turn down your sheets and put a mint on your pillow. I decided I would do that for her, also. Except I couldn't find a mint. I looked all over the house for something sweet, but there wasn't anything. Finally, I grabbed a jar of strawberry jelly and put that on her pillow. Then I folded down her sheets.

Magoo would probably give me my dad's job caring for Bark the second she saw what I did!

CHAPTER

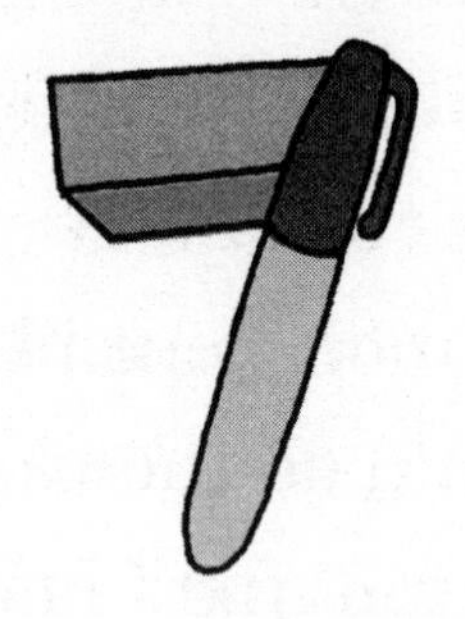

Elliott and I woke up on Saturday to the sun kissing us on our noses. We still couldn't believe our luck that we got to sleep inside *and* outside, almost. We shuffled into the kitchen just as my dad whistled for Bark to come take his walk. He came running with his big tail wagging.

Dad clipped the leash to his collar and I couldn't believe that even with the turned down bed and strawberry jelly on Magoo's pillow, I still had to take care of the **stinky** cats. Dad said if Elliott and I wanted to come along, we should hurry up and feed the cats and put on our coats.

Outside, I memorized how he held the leash just in case his wrist stopped working and I needed to take his place. Then I memorized exactly the streets we walked down so that I wouldn't get lost when I finally got to take care of Bark myself.

"You are such a good Labradinger," I said to Bark. That is when Elliott pointed to the little dog rounding the corner running toward us. Then not even two seconds after, another person with their dog rounded the corner and then even more.

"What is going on over there?" my

dad asked. "It's like an animal parade."
Then a rabbit on a leash appeared. And then a cat on a leash! We walked really fast to the corner and, when we got there, we saw even more people with their pets.

"Maybe it's an audition for animal TV!" Elliott said.

"Anything's possible," my dad said.
We got closer. Finally when we got close enough, I read the sign. You will never in **one million** decades guess what it said.

VETERINARIAN'S OFFICE!

My dad looked me right in the eyes and that's how he knew exactly what I was thinking.

"Don't even think about it, Bird."

"Just for one half of a centimeter of a second?" I begged him.

"No. We have way too much to do. There are vets in Chester. You can wait until we get back home."

We weren't getting back home for another entire full day and a little! That was nearly **foreverteen** hours!

I dragged my feet and hung my head extra low on the walk back so my dad would know just how sad I was.

When we got back to Magoo's, Elliott and I saw her crutches leaning against the wall. We looked at each other. Maybe she was healed? Then two seconds later, Magoo rolled down the hall. She was in a wheelchair!

That is when I stopped breathing almost **forever**. I could not believe my **worldwide** eyes! Elliott was freeze-tagged into place.

For a second I thought Magoo

broke something else, but then she explained that she just needed to get off her foot for a while. Also the crutches made her armpits hurt. I knew that I would *never* get hurt armpits if I had crutches.

I thought walking on her silver crutches would be the most fun thing in the world. But when I saw the wheelchair, I changed it to the second most wonderful thing in the world.

Pushing Magoo in her wheelchair would be the most **extremely, honestly, number one-tastic, most official thing** that I ever did. If I showed Magoo how natural I was at pushing a wheelchair, she would know how good I was at taking care of people. And if I was good at taking care of people, then I'd probably be good at taking care of dogs. People are bigger than dogs.

"Do you need me to push you somewhere?" I asked her.

"No, I'm good where I am, sweetie. Thanks, though."

"Oh," I answered, disappointed. "Maybe you need me to walk on your crutches so they don't get stale?"

She laughed. "I think my crutches are okay."

"Because I know for a scientific fact that if you leave things out for too long they can go stale."

"Frannie," my dad warned.

"What?"

"You *know* what."

"I don't! I don't know what!" I argued.

"Aunt Magoo's wheelchair and

crutches are off-limits," my mom called from the couch where she was reading the newspaper.

Oh yeah, ***that*** what.

"Don't you worry about my crutches. I think they'll be just fine on their own."

That is not a fact **I** agreed with.

I walked over to the wheelchair and stood next to her. She was busy making a sock doll and wasn't paying so much attention to my *please can **I** wear your crutches* expression. Or even my ***I'm** probably the best wheelchair pusher-er in the world* face.

Elliott sat on the other side of Magoo, working on his own sock doll. They were being very concentrate-y and quiet. They were also being boring.

I put my hand on the handlebar part of the chair.

"Well, if you *did* need someone to push you, I bet I'd be really good at it," I told her.

Magoo looked up and smiled. "You know what? I would love it if you could push me into the kitchen so I could get a glass of water."

"OKAY!" I said. I was almost as excited as I was when I got to drive a bumper car. I got behind Magoo's chair and pushed it very slowly into the kitchen. It was much heavier than I thought it would be, but still, I was a very good wheelchair roller. I stood next to Magoo as she drank her water and then I pushed her back to the exact place she had been before.

"Do you need more water?" I asked.

"I just drank some, silly!"

"When you break something you get very thirsty," I told her.

"Really, is that a fact?" Magoo wanted to know.

"Oh," I responded, looking down. "Well, maybe not a *scientific* fact," I said.

"I'll let you know if I want more water."

"Okay, but if you need me to push you somewhere else really soon," I told her, "I could do that, too."

"Sounds like a deal," she said.

I waited. And waited. **And waited**. But Magoo didn't need to go anywhere. Then I got bored and decided to count how many rooms (including bathrooms and closets) Magoo had in her house.

When I went into Magoo's room, she yelled, "The boxes are off-limits!"

"Okay," I yelled back, even though I didn't know what she was talking about.

But then I saw them. There were three very big cardboard boxes, one next to the other. I went over to look.

One was filled with cloth and yarn, the next with buttons, and the next with socks and cotton! Because they were "off-limits," **I looked with my eyes and not with my hands**, as my dad would say.

Next to the boxes was a bag. Its mouth was wide open. I stood over it and looked inside and you would not believe what was in it!

It was filled with a hospital amount of medical tape, Ace bandages, Band-Aids, and every single thing in the world that you could ever imagine or want. I didn't know which bag I liked more, my dad's briefcase or this one. I pulled it out and brought it with me into the living room to show everyone. It was not a box so it was okay that **I** looked with my hands.

"Look what I found!" I said.

Everyone looked at the bag.

"What is that?" my dad asked.

"It's supplies for my leg," Magoo explained.

"Frannie, where did you find that?" my dad asked in his ***I'm a little bit annoyed with you*** voice.

"It's not a box!" I argued.

"Frannie," continued my dad, "put that bag back immediately. You know you don't go through other people's personal belongings. You leave Magoo's things alone, okay? The Ace bandages, the medical tape, the crutches, the wheelchair, it's all off-limits. Do you understand? We need your help with the cats, not with the medical supplies."

"Fine," I **grumped**, and then dragged the bag back to Magoo's room, sat on her bed, and waited to become unbored.

CHAPTER

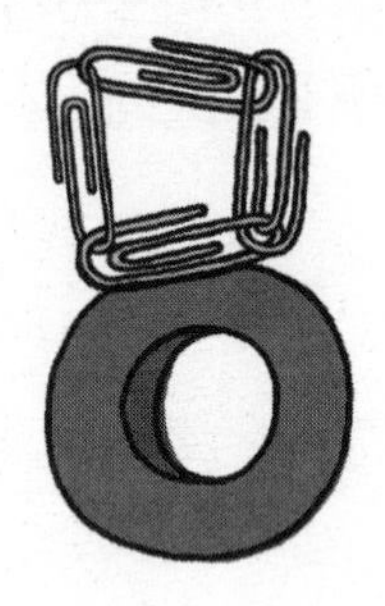

After we cleaned all the dishes from dinner, we got to do whatever it was we wanted until bedtime. Magoo still had to work on her dolls because tomorrow was the big day with the fancy toy store person. Now she had company, though. Elliott was working so hard on his sock doll, it was almost done! He was so good at it, I worried he might not want to be my secretary, after all.

"Frannie, would you like to start a new doll?" Magoo asked. "I can thread a needle if you need help."

"That's okay," I told her.

Making sock dolls is fun but I needed to concentrate on showing Magoo how responsible and thoughtful I am. Which is why I went looking again for something mintish to put on her pillow.

I still couldn't find anything so I took a big jar of honey and put *that* on her pillow. The jelly from the day before was on her night table so I left it there.

Then I looked over and saw her crutches leaning up against her wall, looking very lonely. If Magoo wasn't going to use them, I didn't understand why I couldn't. They were just going to waste lying there against the wall like that. And also they were probably going stale.

I tiptoed down the hall and saw my mom and dad talking in the kitchen while they drank tea. Magoo and Elliott were busy with their dolls. This was the absolute perfect time! No one would even see me use the crutches so they would never even know that I used them, which meant I could **never** get in trouble!

I tiptoed back to Magoo's room and shut her door. As I walked toward the crutches, I heard a sound at the door. I opened it and there was Bark! He was always trying to tell everyone that he wanted me to be in charge of him instead of my dad. But no one understood this except for me because **no one really understood Bark the way I did**. I let him in the room and then I shut the door again.

The crutches were really tall. I wasn't sure how my armpits would reach the top. That was when I decided to drag the crutches over to the bed. Then I stood on the bed and set the crutches in a ready position. I leaned over and placed my armpits on the cushiony top part. Then, when both armpits were in their seats, I stepped off the bed. **But then something horrible happened**. My feet did not touch the floor and I was swinging by my armpits from the crutches.

Bark came over to help me, but he knocked into the crutches, which slipped out from under me and I fell right on top of him. Bark yelped very loudly and leaped away, banging into the night table and knocking the picture frames and the jar of jelly to

the floor. The crutches crashed into the wall and then plunked down to the floor next to them, and I landed on my butt with a bang. There were **three million** different crashes, which is why the door flew open and I saw the **extremely worried** faces of my mom, dad, and Elliott.

"Are you okay?" my mother asked as she ran to help me up on my feet.

As soon as I told her I was fine, my dad's face filled with red, splotchy anger. Elliott put his hand over his mouth and my mom put her hands on her waist, which is what she does when she is about to yell at me. **I was in a worldwide canyon of trouble**.

CHAPTER

After I fell off the crutches, my dad and mom had to think of an "appropriate" punishment for me. When they came back they told me that my punishment was that I could no longer go with my dad to pick up the **fancy** toy store woman.

"What about Elliott?" I asked.

"He'll have to stay behind as well," said my mother. Elliott was really mad about this because he wanted to show her his doll and make her **impresstified** by his natural talents. I apologized to Elliott **ten thousandteen** times, but he went to bed mad.

When I woke up on Sunday, I went into the kitchen where my parents and Magoo were eating breakfast. Everyone was still upset with me because I only got a very soft "Good morning." And not even one "How did you sleep?"

Elliott came out and rubbed the sleep from his eyes. When he opened them, he looked at me and said, "I'm still a little mad at you."

That gave me a bad feeling, but I understood.

"Sorry, Elliott," I said again.

"Okay, kids," my dad said,

clapping his hands together. "We have a very big morning upon us. Elliott and Frannie, we need to hop to it. I need the two of you to vacuum the floors and the couches. When I leave to pick up the toy store woman, I need you to shut Hester, Lester, Esther, and Bark up tightly in the television room. Okay?"

We nodded.

"Mom is going to pick up some nice sandwiches for Magoo's big meeting. While we're gone, I want you to take care of Magoo. Wait on her hand and foot, okay? Whatever she needs or wants, you get it for her. Understand?"

At least we still had jobs to do. Which meant it wasn't too late to show how responsible I was.

Then we got to work. Elliott and

I held the long hose of the vacuum cleaner with all of our hands just to make it steady. It took **forty million hours** to get the cat hair off everything. Once we did that, we had to clean the entire floor!

When we were done, Elliott and I were out of all our breath. We took a little break, but soon our break turned boring since we couldn't do anything because it might mess up the house.

When my parents left, Elliott and I rounded up all the animals and put them in the television room. It was really hard to get each cat in there because they meowed and slipped away every time we'd go to catch them. Once we got all three cats into the television room, Bark followed them and we shut the door very tightly behind us.

If you can even believe it, things got even **boringer**. Magoo said she was going to do fifteen minutes of a *very quiet* exercise called meditation. That meant she was going to sit very still in her meditation room and we had to be **very, very quiet**. Sitting still did not sound like exercise to me.

"You just need to be quiet for fifteen minutes. Do you think you can do that?" Magoo asked.

"Yes!" we told Magoo.

"You can keep the animals company and watch some television quietly. Okay?"

"We'll be very quiet," I told her. Then she crutched her way into the meditation room where **she did an exercise that was not an exercise at all**.

Elliott and I went into the television room and roamed around for a good channel, which was not very hard to find since Magoo had **one hundred thousand** channels. We sat back on Magoo's couch and watched a show on Animal Planet. Bark got up and walked over to Hester, Esther, and Lester, and plopped down next to them. That's when I noticed he was walking funny.

"Elliott," I loud-whispered so we didn't break Magoo out of her meditation.

"What?"

"Bark is limping!"

"He is?"

"Yes! Look at the way he's walking."

Bark was now sitting, so I pulled him up to his feet but he just stood there. I pushed him toward Elliott and whisper-shouted, "Bark! Bark! Go to Elliott. Walk to Elliott!"

And after **foreverteen and a day**, he finally made it over to Elliott and then plopped himself down.

"Did you see it?"

Elliott shook his head no.

"Come on, Bark. Let's take a walk and show Elliott how limpish you are." Then I stood and walked around the room very slowly until Bark got up and followed me.

"See it, Elliott?"

"What's it supposed to look like?" Elliott asked, staring at Bark's legs.

"A limp. You know . . ." And then I limped to show him what a limp looked like. Elliott scrunched up his face and got on all fours and watched very closely as Bark followed me some more.

"Are you sure, Frannie? I don't see the limp."

"Maybe we have to look closer." Then I sat down next to Elliott and patted my lap until Bark came to me. I picked up his paw and showed Elliott.

"Do you see the limp now?" I asked him. He stared really hard at the paw.

"I . . . I . . . I'm not sure. Maybe."

That's when I understood that Elliott couldn't see it because he wasn't a dog veterinarian! But **I** *was* and that's why **I** had to **officially** explain to Elliott what was the matter.

"He has a case of limp paw."

"Is that bad?"

"Yes, it could lead to broken paw."

"Is that worse?"

"It's what Magoo has, but on humans."

"What do we do?"

"Well, since I'm almost a real veterinarian, but not yet, we should probably take him to the real one down the street."

"But I don't think we're allowed to do that," Elliott said.

"Well, how else are we supposed to learn how to fix him if we don't go?"

"I don't know," he answered.

"How will you know how to be my secretary?"

"I don't know," he said again.

"And how in the worldwide of America will I learn how to fix such a bad case of limp paw if we don't go right now so I can learn?"

Elliott scrunched his face up into a thinking expression.

"You're probably right," he said. "It *does* make sense. And parents like when you do learning experience type things."

"Right," I agreed.

"So maybe it's a good idea."

"It's a fantastical idea!" **I** said, even though it was my idea and **it's almost like bragging but not quite** to agree that your own idea is **fantastical**.

"We'll take him to the veterinarian and by the time Magoo is done with her meditation, Bark will be fixed and we'll be smarter about limp paw and secretary phones."

"How do we get him there with a broken paw?" Elliott asked.

This was such a good question that I did not correct him that it was limp paw and not broken paw.

We were both **stumpified** as to how to get Bark to the veterinarian. We **harrumphed** our faces and scratched our heads until, finally, I knew exactly how to get him there.

I motioned to the corner where Magoo's wheelchair was folded up. Elliott got up and, almost like he was a professional wheelchair opener, he unfolded it perfectly!

Then we tried very hard to get Bark to jump in and sit. He was not the easiest dog in the world to steer. First we just got his front paws on before he jumped off. Then we got his back paws on before he went skidding off. He was just as slippy as the cats! And that's when I got a **genius-al** idea!

I held up one finger to Elliott, which meant, ***wait one minute***! Then, I ran into the living room where we left Magoo's medical bag and I took out the biggest Ace bandage ever.

We decided that the only way Bark would sit in the chair was if Elliott sat on it first.

"Wait!" Elliott whisper-shouted before he got in. "I want to bring my sock doll so I can finish it while we wait!" He went to the couch, grabbed the sock doll and the thread, and stuck them in his front pocket. Then he got into the wheelchair and we managed to get Bark onto his lap and I wound and wound and wound the Ace bandage all around them. Then I wheeled them out the front door and onto the sidewalk. I very carefully shut the front door behind us. It wasn't until we were halfway down the block that I realized I forgot to write a note. It was okay, though. We'd certainly be back before Dad and the toy store lady got home.

I pushed Elliott and Bark down the sidewalk and people smiled and waved at us. Bark was having a great time. Then we rounded the corner and saw a lot more people with their animals waving at us and smiling. Walking a dog was really fun!

When we got to the veterinarian's office, we had to ring a little bell that sounded like a bird chirping. Then we were buzzed in. It was too hard to hold the door open and push the chair through at the same time so someone in the waiting room had to come out and help us.

I wanted to tell the secretary that we were here, but there wasn't anyone sitting at the front desk.

The waiting room was filled with so many people and animals, it looked like a circus! But I knew it was worth it for me to wait. Once we saw the doctor and he agreed that Bark had limp paw, my family would be so **impresstified**, they would forget all about the crutch incident. Everyone would see what a natural I was with dogs, and they would let me quit school to become a veterinarian!

CHAPTER 10

Since there were no seats left in the waiting room, I wheeled Bark and Elliott to the corner near a plant. Then I tried to memorize every detail of the veterinarian's office so I could copy it at my practice veterinarian's office at home.

A teenage boy holding a soda can looked over at us.

"Cool wheelchair," he said.

Elliott and I looked at each other and smiled. We never really had teenagers talk to us **ever**. And we never had one tell us we were cool.

"Thanks," I said. "He can't walk because of his limp paw," I explained.

"Totally cool," said the teenage boy.

What a good day this was turning out to be!

"It's not so comfortable," Elliott said to the teenager. He and Bark were still Ace bandaged into the wheelchair. He looked up at me. "Can we get out?"

"I guess so," I said. I untied the back end of the Ace bandage and unwound and unwound. Then, when it was totally unwound, the front door opened and a woman with two dogs came into the office. I giggled a little on the inside of my brain because the dogs looked exactly like each other.

I guess Bark loves dogs that look exactly like each other because that was when he jumped out of Elliott's lap and raced right for the door. The dogs got very scared, even though I know for a **scientific fact** that Bark just wanted to play with them.

Suddenly, a **shriekish** type of sound came from each of the dogs at exactly the same time. Their owner pulled back on the leashes, but Bark went barreling right toward them! On the way, he knocked into the other animals and also the people sitting there waiting to see the veterinarian.

A woman had her newspaper knocked out of her hands. The teenage boy who had talked to us got his soda knocked out of his hand, and the brown liquid landed in splats all over his jeans.

Rabbits and cats pawed and scratched at their cages and we could hear loud flapping bird wings and a **millionteen** squawk-squawk-squawks. It sounded like a big waiting room storm. Elliott and I stood there **stumpified** for one second. Then I figured out that since we were the ones Bark came with, we were the ones who had to find him and stop the **hurricane of craziosity**.

"Bark!" I yelled, and then went to look down the hall where I heard even more squawking and barking

and meowing and even human voices yelling, "Where's the dog's owner?" "Has anyone seen my rabbit?" "Here, kitty, kitty." "Someone's going to pay for this!"

I was in so much trouble!

Finally, Bark ran out of one room and across the hall into another. Elliott and I ran toward that room and as soon as we got there, Bark ran out and into another. He was being really wild and running so fast we couldn't catch him. Then Bark ran into a room and Elliott and I stopped in our tracks when we heard the clanking sound of tools being dropped and things crashing to the floor. It was not the best moment of the world, **and that is not an opinion**.

A doctor ran out of his doctor room and shouted, "What on earth is going on?! Who is responsible for this animal?"

Elliott and I didn't know what to do because we weren't *really* responsible for Bark **although at this very exact moment in time we probably scientifically were**. So, finally, I raised my hand very slowly and in a very quiet mouse voice, I said, "I am."

The doctor was calming Bark down with a treat and petting him. Bark was being on his best behavior now. Then a secretary walked out of a different doctor room and stood over us.

"And who, exactly, is responsible for you?"

"Dan and Anna Miller," I told them.

"Well, can you please tell us how to get in touch with them?" The secretary seemed very, very angry. As I told her my mom's cell phone number, I started to get a **very bad day feeling** on my skin.

"Why don't you wait on the bench outside while I call your mother, okay?" the angry secretary said.

Elliott and I looked at each other with big, worried faces. Then Elliott took Bark by the leash and I followed them into the waiting room where I got the wheelchair and we headed out the front door. But before we left, I turned to everyone in the waiting room and said sorry to the ground, even though it was meant for the people.

When we got outside, Elliott got back into the wheelchair, we got Bark on his lap, and I wrapped them with the Ace bandage. Then, just as I was about to sit on the bench in front of the veterinarian's office, my mom rounded the corner with a **very bad day mood** on her face.

And just as she went to open her mouth to let us know how much trouble we were in, her cell phone rang.

"Hello? What? No! Oh my! That's just—Okay, okay, okay. We'll be right there." Then she hung up the phone, looked at us, and said, "Come on kids, we have to hurry!" She raced ahead, rounded the corner, and ran to the end of the block where Magoo lived.

I pushed Bark and Elliott very quickly but also very professionally around the corner and up the block behind my mother. It was **exhaustifying**. By the time we got to

Magoo's house, my chest was all out of breath.

Just as my mom was about to open the front door, it flew open and a very large woman with tears in her very red eyes, a swollen face, and red bumps on her neck came running out. Magoo came crutching up to the door behind her yelling, "Wait! Wait! We can do this somewhere else!" And then I saw the slippy cats on the floor behind them.

When I saw the cats, that's when I got a **very bad feeling** in my memory. And that bad feeling was that when I pushed the wheelchair out of the television room, I might have, maybe, perhaps, possibly, it could be, there's a little chance that by the **hugest of accidents**, I left the door just a little bit open.

Maybe.

The big lady stopped when she saw us. I looked behind her and saw Magoo and Dad's bright red, angry faces. My mom was standing next to us, and her face was angry, too.

Elliott and I froze like Popsicles. The lady stood right over us, with her hands on her hips. And we stared up at her, terrified. But then, she did the weirdest thing in the entire world.

She laughed.

I didn't know what she thought was so funny. Looking at all the very mad faces glaring at us from inside Magoo's house, you'd think there'd never be anything funny ever again.

"Who are you and what in the world are you doing?" she asked.

"I'm Frannie and this is my best

MAIL

friend, Elliott. And that's Bark. We thought he had a case of limp paw so we took him to the veterinarian around the corner."

"And you brought him in a wheelchair?"

"He had limp paw! He couldn't walk!" Elliott said.

"What's that you have there?" the lady asked, pointing to Elliott's pocket. He looked down and pulled out his sock doll.

"This is my sock doll."

"Did Margot make that for you?"

"No, I'm making it."

"*You're* making it?"

"Yes. And when it's done, it's going to be my good luck charm."

The woman didn't say anything for a minute. Then she turned around and looked at Magoo with brand-new eyes and asked, "Is there a drugstore nearby?"

"Just across the street from the vet's office," Magoo told her.

The lady looked at me and Elliott and asked, "Can you take me there?"

We looked at my dad, who shrugged.

"Okay," I said.

Then the lady turned to Magoo and said, "You put the cats away. I'm going to get some allergy medicine, then I'll come back. I think these children just gave me a marvelous idea about your dolls."

Elliott and I left Bark and the wheelchair with Mom, Dad, and Magoo. They all looked half confused and half the maddest I've ever seen them in my **worldwide life** and that is **very**, **extremely**, **professionally** mad.

We each took one of the lady's hands and went to the drugstore. She picked out some medicine and also some eyedrops. As soon as she put the drops in her eyes, the red magically disappeared. She told us the splotches and bumps would go away about twenty minutes after she took the other medicine. Then we headed back to Magoo's to hear her *marvelous* idea.

CHAPTER 11

When we got back, my parents had on their "you are in the hugest amount of trouble but we are in front of company so you are not getting punished at this exact minute" expressions.

They had to keep these expressions for a long time since the fancy lady wanted me and Elliott to stay and hear her *marvelous* idea. She gave a long, boring talk about the dolls and said words that had *Q*s in them, so we knew whatever they meant was complicated.

Then she said things about other dolls and other toys and even though she was talking about dolls and toys, I can tell you for a **scientific fact** that it was **not** interesting. But when she started talking about me and Elliott, suddenly it became interesting.

"When I saw these kids and that little boy with his handmade doll, I had a vision."

Magoo was leaning in so closely, I saw the little hairs on my arms rise and fall from her breath.

"Not only are we going to sell your dolls, but we're going to do workshops where we teach children how to knit, crochet, sew, and . . . with your permission, make your sock dolls."

Magoo inhaled the biggest breath of happiness.

"Really?" she asked.

"Yes, really. I know that the children will love it!" Then she said things that sounded like this: *Boring boring boring. Even more boring. The boringest of boring. Something so boring it bores even the most boring things in the entire world.* ***One last thing that is so boring, I just bored my own self to sleep.*** I'd like to start as soon as possible. Do you think you could have one hundred dolls in the store by September?"

"Absolutely. It would be my honor," Magoo said.

The fancy toy store woman stood, shook hands with Magoo, gave me and Elliott each a big kiss, and thanked us. And then Mom, Dad, and Magoo

walked and crutched their way to the door. When they came back, Elliott and I stood up, very happy and on our way to play in the other room. My dad put his arm out and rested it on my shoulder.

"Not so fast, Frances."

CHAPTER 12

We were in a **Frances** amount of trouble. When my parents use my full name, Frances, **it's serious**.

We didn't know that we had left the door open behind us when we went to get the wheelchair. So we didn't know that the cats got out, and that Magoo couldn't get them back in the room because she was on crutches. We also didn't know that time went by so fast. What we did know was that we left the house without an adult and that we were just *very* lucky that the fancy toy store lady had a **genius-al** brain and got a good idea just from seeing Elliott with that doll.

We had so much to fix in order to make things right again that I almost lost track.

First, we had to apologize to Magoo. We went into Magoo's room, and she was sitting on her bed, making a brand-new sock doll.

"Magoo?" I said.

"Mmmmm. . . .?" she replied with a needle clamped between her teeth.

"Elliott and I wanted to tell you that we're sorry we almost ruined your life."

Magoo looked up with a smile, but didn't say anything back.

"We were only trying to help because we thought that Bark had limp paw."

"Well, it's nice that you wanted to pitch in, but it sure did cause me a lot of stress," Magoo said.

"I'm sorry."

"I know you are, honey. I would just ask that, in the future, you'll think long and hard before you make a decision. Because if your decision affects other people in a bad way, maybe it's not a good decision."

I looked down at the ground. "Does that mean I was selfish?"

"I'm afraid so," she said.

"I'm sorry, Aunt Magoo. I really didn't mean to be selfish on purpose. I got excited."

"Oh, it's okay, as long as you

learned from it for next time. Now come here both of you." We went over to Magoo and she wrapped us up in her arms and hugged us. When we were walking out of the room, she stopped us and we turned around.

"Thank you," she said.

"For what?" I asked.

"For being you. After all, none of this would have happened if it hadn't been for the two of you."

Elliott and I shrugged. Who else were we supposed to be?

Then Dad walked us over to the veterinarian's office where we apologized to everybody and stayed for one entire hour helping them clean up. I was very worried that we had scared all the animals for the rest of their **worldwide** lives.

But the secretary said they were all going to be fine, **and that is not an opinion**.

When everything was cleaned up, the secretary showed Elliott how to work the phone bank since he was going to be a veterinarian's secretary. And the veterinarian let me try on his stethoscope and white jacket! It was all **very official** and **definitely** and **clearly professional**.

When we got home, my mom said that even though we had made a lot of apologies, saying we were sorry was not enough. What else in the **worldwide of America** could we do, I wondered?

First, we were not allowed to watch any more TV. We had to go to bed one half hour earlier and read to ourselves instead of being read to. *And* we had to give Hester, Esther, and Lester baths. And if you think cats are slippy when they're dry, you should never wash a cat!

It was the worst day of my entire life, but it was also the best. I was with my best friend in the world, I got to wear a real veterinarian's jacket and a stethoscope, my aunt sold her dolls, and Elliott's sock doll was already lucky charmed!

Everything worked out in the end.

Except that I was not allowed to quit school and become a veterinarian.

Not yet, anyway.

THE END.

About the Author

AJ Stern lives in an upside-down house in Brooklyn, NY. She has fifteen children under the age of eleven who all have very good jobs. She rides to work on a horse and only eats food that is orange. Okay, none of this is true (except the Brooklyn part), but it would be a little funny if it were. Right?

About the Illustrator

After graduating from Carnegie Mellon University, Doreen Mulryan Marts worked at Marvel Comics as a production assistant and as a product designer for Russ Berrie. Now she works as a freelance illustrator and designer from the comfort of her New Jersey home.